LISTEN TO THE STORYTELLER

A TRIO OF MUSICAL TALES FROM AROUND THE WORLD

ILLUSTRATED BY KRISTEN BALOUCH

With *an introduction by*

WYNTON MARSALIS

VIKING

IN MEMORY OF MILES GOODMAN

Viking Children's Books and Sony Classical gratefully acknowledge the contributions of
Patrick Doyle, Wynton Marsalis, and Edgar Meyer to *Listen to the Storyteller*

To my mom and dad and our very interesting journeys

—K. B.

*While the stories in this book contain themes, characters, and situations reminiscent
of folktale traditions found throughout the world, each tale is wholly original and
was conceived in a collaborative effort between Sony Classical and
Viking Children's Books specifically for this project.*

VIKING
Published by the Penguin Group
Penguin Putnam Inc., 345 Hudson Street, New York, New York 10014, U.S.A.

Penguin Books Ltd, Registered Offices: Harmondsworth, Middlesex, England

First published in 1999 by Viking, a division of Penguin Putnam Books for Young Readers

1 3 5 7 9 10 8 6 4 2

LIBRARY OF CONGRESS CATALOGING-IN-PUBLICATION DATA
Listen to the storyteller: a trio of musical tales from around the world /
illustrations by Kristen Balouch ; with an introduction by Wynton Marsalis.
p.   cm.
Contents: The lesson of the land (Native American) — The face in the lake (Celtic) —
The fiddler and the dancin' witch (Afro-Caribbean)
Summary: A collection of three original tales derived from diverse
cultural and folktale traditions.
ISBN 0-670-88054-X
1. Fairy tales. [1. Fairy tales.] I. Balouch, Kristen, ill
PZ8.L687 1999 [E]—DC21 97-43615 CIP AC

Printed in U.S.A. • Set in Minister

INTRODUCTION

Everyone loves to hear a good story. Storytellers take us into worlds wondrous and unknown. They tell us how life is, was, and perhaps will be. Whether a story is ancient or new, scary, sad, or funny, it's even better when spoken out loud—yes, much better. Because when someone tells the tale out loud, we can feel the storyteller's love for the story. And for us, too. And that's wonderful.

Music makers have their own ways of telling a story. They use melody, rhythm, and the sounds made by different instruments to bring out parts of a story that are sometimes hidden in the telling. Music helps us feel, understand, and remember what the storyteller is saying. It's like ketchup on some french fries: they're still french fries, but that ketchup makes us feel a different way about them.

But whether a story is told with words, with music, or with both, all we need to do is use our ears and our imagination. So let's prepare to enter a magical world filled with witches and castles, escapes and adventures, transformations and tests of courage. Gather round now, and listen to the storyteller. . . .

THE FIDDLER AND THE DANCIN' WITCH

HUSH now children and listen to the tale I'm goin' to tell.

There once was an old man, and that old man, he had himself a son named Simeon. Together they lived in a little village on an island in a deep green sea.

Now, Simeon was a good boy, but he had a mind of his own. Couldn't tell him a thing, that boy.

"You got ears to hear with," his father told him. "So you better listen good when your elders are talkin' to you!"

But Simeon was a hard-headed boy. So he said, "Ears are good for lots of things 'sides listenin' to grownups!"

"Such as?" his father asked.

"Ears are good for listenin' to music!" answered Simeon. "Like that music you sometimes play on your fiddle late at night when you think I'm sleepin'."

"What are you doin' listenin' to me play the fiddle?" asked his father.

"I just want to learn how to play the way you do," answered Simeon. "Won't you teach me, please?"

But the old man wouldn't hear of it. "That is no ordinary kind of fiddle," he said. "It's a *magic* kind of fiddle, and no one but me can play it, or there'll be trouble, trouble, and more trouble."

But did that hard-headed boy care about trouble? No indeed! He begged and pleaded with his father every day from dawn to dusk till the old man got so tired of his naggin' he gave in and let the boy pick up the fiddle.

Thing was, that fiddle had a mind of its own, too. So the first thing that came out when Simeon started playin' was that same enchantin' music he'd heard his father play so many times.

Now, Simeon loved that pretty music, but he couldn't help wonderin', where was the trouble, trouble, and more trouble his daddy had talked about? And sure enough, just as soon as he started thinkin' those thoughts, that fiddle started makin' some mighty strange, bewitchin' music.

When his father heard it, he snatched that fiddle away.

"Listen to what I'm tellin' you," said the old man. "That's the kind of music that will call out a witch just as sure as I'm standin' here. Now don't you

ever go touchin' my fiddle again, 'less I
say you can."

But that stubborn boy was only listenin'
with one ear. He was too busy wonderin'
how that fiddle knew to play whatever he was
thinkin'.

Now Simeon *tried* to obey his father, but you know
how stories go. There's always one thing the hero is not supposed to do. And
bang—just like that, that's the very first thing he always does.

So sure enough, one day when his father had gone out to work in the cane
fields, Simeon could feel that fiddle callin' out to him. And when he found
where his father had hidden it away, Simeon just couldn't help but pick it up
and start playin' some wild music.

Right away the *strangest* things began to happen.

A fierce wind started blowin' through the trees. Dark clouds rushed in and
blocked out the sun. Dogs in the village started meowin', and cats started in
to bark. Soon all the neighbors ran out of their houses to see what was causin'
such a commotion, but stopped short when they saw a big gray cloud whirlin'
and twirlin' and fixin' to settle down right in front of Simeon's house.

Then out of that cloud popped the nastiest old witch you'd ever want to
lay eyes on. The neighbors shrieked and stepped back, and even Simeon had
to stop his fiddlin'. That old witch walked right up to him and said, "That
fiddle belongs to me, boy. Your daddy stole it from me a long time ago, and I

ain't been able to dance my witch's dance ever since. But now I aim to get it back!"

Well, that stubborn boy just looked at her, cool as a cucumber, and said, "My daddy's an honest man. If he got that fiddle from you, he got it fair and square. And if you want it back, *you're* gonna have to get it fair and square, too!"

"Oh, foolish boy," said the witch. "I'll tell you what. If you can play that fiddle longer and stronger than I can dance my dance, I'll let you keep it, and I promise I'll never show my face around these parts again."

"And if I can't?" asked Simeon.

"Then I'll take back my fiddle," she answered. "And because you're such a sassy boy, I'll take something else, too—your ears!"

The neighbors gasped, but that

willful boy just answered, "Ha! You'll never get my ears! I'll fiddle till you drop!"

And so the music started. That mean old witch started in dancin' as fast and as furious as any witch ever danced.

The music got louder and louder, till even Simeon's father could hear it way, way off in the cane fields. And the old man knew that wild music meant only one thing—trouble, trouble, and more trouble!

Off he ran to the village. When he got there he stopped dead in his tracks to find that nasty old witch dancin' away in his own front yard and Simeon playin' the fiddle like a house on fire.

"Boy, you better listen to me now," Simeon's father yelled. But Simeon was too scared to stop and listen, for fear he'd lose his ears. So he just kept on fiddlin' faster and faster, till that magic fiddle got so hot it glowed like a fiery red poker in his hands.

Soon the old man saw that his son was startin' to look mighty worn out. But that rotten old witch kept dancin' and prancin', whirlin' and twirlin' like she could go on all night.

So Simeon's father did the only thing he could— he started in clappin' his hands, stompin' his feet, and hollerin' for Simeon to keep on playin'. "Come on now, son!" he shouted, and soon all the neighbors joined in clappin', stompin', and hollerin', too.

Simeon was mighty scared now, so he started playin' faster, crazier, and wilder than ever. And that witch was keepin' up, too, dancin' and spinnin' quicker and quicker till the neighbors started gettin' dizzy just watchin' her. Then suddenly, her feet sputtered with sparks. Her hair stood on end. And all at once, she spun herself 'round so fast she turned into a whirlin' tornado and disappeared with a great big *whoosh*!

Simeon stopped fiddlin'. He felt for his ears and grinned a grin from ear to ear to find they were still there on either side of his head.

The wind died down, the sun came out from behind the clouds, the dogs stopped meowin', and the cats stopped barkin'. The neighbors let out a big sigh of relief and cheered the boy for savin' their town from the witch.

Simeon was so worn out he walked right over to his father and ever so politely handed him the fiddle.

"You are one willful son," his father said. "But I'll tell you, that was the best fiddle playin' I ever did hear."

"That fiddle played whatever I thought," said Simeon. "And I had to do some mighty quick thinkin' to beat that witch. But I'll tell you what. I'll never again play that fiddle when you're not around, I promise."

Well, Simeon kept his promise, and that nasty old witch was never seen in those parts again. And ever since that day children from that little village on an island in a deep green sea always prick up their ears—and listen real good—whenever their elders say, "You got ears to hear with, so you better listen to what I'm sayin!"

You hear?

THE LESSON OF THE LAND

NIGHT had fallen, and the darkening sky shimmered with stars. The men of the tribe could be heard singing to the Great Mystery and to the spirits of powerful animals, praying to be granted their wisdom. At sunrise, three young friends would set forth to do what boys of their tribe had always done to become men—they would go on a journey to seek visions from the animal spirits who would guide them through life.

Eagle Son, Little Bear, and Running Wolf huddled together in the darkness, listening to the prayers of the elders. "Tomorrow," said Eagle Son, "we will travel to the world beyond our world. No matter what struggles lie before us, we must find the strength in ourselves to follow the wisdom of our elders—to respect the land who is our mother and to honor the animal people who are our brothers. Only then will we be ready to receive our visions."

At dawn, the three met at the edge of the village. Eagle Son stood proud and strong, ready to lead the way. Little Bear stumbled along sleepily, while Running Wolf arrived last, clutching his knife fiercely.

The three friends set out for the mountains at the farthest slope of their valley. As they made their way up the rocky mountainside, Running Wolf and Little Bear complained of the steep climb and the sharp thorns that scratched their legs. But Eagle Son urged them on, stopping only to help Little Bear when he fell behind. Finally they reached the summit and looked out upon the vast prairie that stretched below them.

"I'm tired," whimpered Little Bear.

"We will stop here for the night," said Eagle Son. He gathered dried grass and soon started a fire, while Running Wolf searched about impatiently. "I bet I'll see my spirit guide first," Running Wolf boasted.

All at once Running Wolf called out, "Brothers, I have found food!" When the other boys joined him, they saw a nest built of pebbles, with three very large green eggs in the center. Before the others could stop him, Running Wolf grabbed the eggs and thrust them in the fire.

"No!" cried Eagle Son. "It is not right to eat those strange-looking eggs."

Running Wolf sneered. "You are a fool, Eagle Son. Go hungry if you wish. My belly will be full tonight!"

"Maybe Eagle Son is right. . . ." Little Bear said uncertainly.

"The decision is yours," said Running Wolf, shrugging. "I will gladly eat all three!" And with that, he lifted the eggs from the fire and cut their delicate shells. Eagle Son shook his head sadly as Running Wolf greedily ate all the eggs without even making an offering or saying a prayer.

They lay down for the night in uneasy silence. Eagle Son and Little Bear

had just drifted into a restless sleep when the night was pierced by a shrill cry: "Oh, my brothers, help me!"

The two friends hurried to Running Wolf, who was writhing on the ground, shivering and clutching his stomach. "My belly is on fire," he moaned, "but the rest of me is so cold." The boys quickly covered Running Wolf with blankets and gave him water to drink. Soon his moaning quieted, and his worried friends lay down once more. "I feel s-strange," Running Wolf whispered throughout the night. "S-so s-strange."

Eagle Son awoke early the next morning, troubled by the events of the previous night. Suddenly he felt a shadow pass over him, and looking up he saw a majestic eagle soar across the sky. Eagle Son sat perfectly still as the eagle circled overhead and came to rest on a nearby rock. For a few seconds they stared at each other, then all at once the eagle took flight in the direction of the boys' village and was soon gone from sight. In that moment, Eagle Son knew he had received his vision. He understood that he had done the right thing by refusing to eat the eggs, for in doing so, he had honored the spirits of the animal people.

The morning sun was shining brightly when Eagle Son and Little Bear found Running Wolf trembling beneath his blankets. "Help me," he whispered, "I can't feel my legs." Eagle Son pulled back the blankets and stared in amazement at what lay before them. The skin on Running Wolf's legs had grown rough and scaly and was marked with thin green stripes.

"What should we do?" asked Little Bear, his voice shaking.

Eagle Son remembered his vision of the eagle flying toward their village. "We must turn around and bring Running Wolf home," he answered.

They lifted their friend to his feet, and putting his arms around their shoulders, made their way slowly down the mountain. Running Wolf could only murmur feverishly as they struggled along. "S-s-something is very wrong," he whispered. "I feel s-so s-strange."

The boys walked for hours, but when their village had not come into sight by nightfall, they realized they were lost. In the growing darkness, uncertain of which way to turn, they stopped beside a river. Eagle Son busied himself with making a fire, while Little Bear paced anxiously. "Little Bear," said Eagle Son, "Running Wolf needs our help, and you must do your part, too. Go quickly now and look for food while I stay with him."

Reluctantly, Little Bear made his way to the river. At the water's edge he saw a gleaming fish swim by under the surface, and thrust his hands clumsily into the river. But no matter how many times he tried to grab it, the fish slipped through his fingers.

Little Bear was ready to give up, when he looked across the river and saw a mighty bear staring back at him. The bear then looked into the water, lifted its paw, and in one swift motion scooped a fish from the river. Little Bear tried again, now imitating the great bear, and immediately caught a wriggling fish of his own. He looked up in time to see the bear disappear into the

woods, and in that moment, Little Bear knew he had received his vision. He understood that the strength and grace of the noble bear could be his, giving him the power to help his friends as they had so often helped him.

Little Bear returned to his friends, proudly bearing the fish, only to find Running Wolf complaining of burning pain in his legs. Little Bear helped Eagle Son carry Running Wolf to the river where the cool, rippling waters seemed to soothe Running Wolf's pain. But when the boys returned later to pull Running Wolf onto the bank, they gasped at the sight before them—Running Wolf's legs had grown together into a green tail.

Eagle Son and Little Bear helped their ailing friend to the fire and wrapped him in blankets. All through the night they could hear Running Wolf's faint voice: "My brothers-s, this-s is-s a great les-s-son. . . . S-s-so it must be, s-s-so it must be. . . ."

When morning came, Running Wolf was nowhere to be seen. Eagle Son and Little Bear cautiously drew aside the blankets where he had lain, and froze in disbelief. The Great Mystery had transformed Running Wolf into the very creature whose eggs he had eaten—a long green snake.

Eagle Son and Little Bear stared as the snake raised its head to look at them and then began to glide through the grass. The boys followed curiously and soon realized the snake was guiding them home.

When at last the village came into sight, the snake stopped. Eagle Son and Little Bear watched as the snake slithered away and disappeared into the tall grass. They knew they would not see Running Wolf again except in their dreams, but he would always be their spirit brother, like the majestic eagle and the great bear. And so Eagle Son and Little Bear headed for their village. They had set out for the world beyond their world as boys . . . and had returned as men.

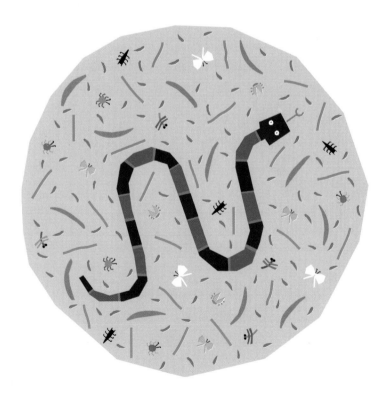

THE FACE IN THE LAKE

ONCE, a very long time ago, when butterflies knew how to sing and the stars whispered to the trees, there lived four siblings who brought forth the seasons to the land. Each year peaceful Olwen delivered springtime, and it was said her gentle kiss could make even the deadwood of bleakest winter burst with fragrant blossoms. One cheerful brother then ripened the fruits of summer, until Olwen's generous sister arrived to preside over the bountiful harvests of autumn.

But the fourth sibling, who was the jealous and cold-hearted master of winter, decided one year to keep the world in his icy clutches forever. So when the time came for spring to return, he surprised his sister Olwen at the crossroads of the four seasons and kidnapped her.

Cruel Winter then cast a spell on Olwen, freezing her power to awaken the tender green of springtime, and brought her to his frozen palace deep in the desolate, forbidding forest. He knew his icy reign would never end as long as Olwen remained locked away, her heart as cold and lonely as his own.

Day after day, Olwen paced in her prison tower while the bravest men in the land tried to free her and win her hand. But each time a daring young suitor approached the castle, Winter sent out his ice gremlins to freeze the unlucky rescuer in his tracks.

Olwen wept bitterly now as she looked down from her tower window upon the frozen suitors who lined the road to the castle. All at once, she heard the fluttering of wings and looked up to see a little wood dove who had braved the dark forest and now perched upon her windowsill.

"Pretty maiden," cooed the wood dove, "do not despair. For it is whispered among the nightbirds that when Olwen falls in love, her brother's spell will melt like snowflakes in the sun."

But before Olwen could respond, the sound of jangling keys outside her door startled the wood dove. "Remember this, dear Olwen," it called to her as it flew away. "See with your heart and not with your eyes."

Just then the door opened, revealing Winter's servant, a small, hunched man named Jardur, whose face was all but hidden by tangled hair and an ice-encrusted beard. Eyes downcast, he shuffled wordlessly into the room carrying a tray of food, as he did each day.

Olwen folded her arms and turned away from him. Unaware that Jardur could not speak, she mistook his silence for cruelty and assumed he was as cold and heartless as his master.

But now as she looked down at the tray in his hands, she was surprised to see a bowl which held a tiny sprig of green. She took the little bud in her hand and tenderly kissed it. Despite her diminished powers, the bud trembled beneath her lips and slowly opened into a blossom. Tears sprang to Olwen's eyes as she beheld this small, hopeful sign of spring.

Olwen looked at Jardur, and saw for the first time that his eyes were not the dull gray she had imagined, but the gentle green eyes of a kind and timid soul—eyes the color of spring.

"Oh, Jardur," said Olwen. "Please forgive me for treating you so coldly. My own anger blinded me from seeing your kindness."

Jardur blushed a bright crimson and looked away shyly.

"Jardur," Olwen said softly, "the life in this tiny blossom means there may still be a chance for spring to return. We must escape and end this terrible winter!"

Jardur's eyes opened wide, and he shook his head fearfully.

"Please," begged Olwen. "You're the only one who can help me." Jardur stared anxiously into her eyes and finally nodded. Taking a deep breath, he moved to the wall, grasped one dark gray stone, and pulled. With a great *whoosh*, the massive stones parted to reveal a secret passageway.

Olwen stared in amazement at the stairway which descended into icy blackness. Jardur took her hand, and together they crept down the steps and

into a long, winding tunnel, hurrying silently toward the dim light of day and the shelter of the dense forest.

Olwen and Jardur fled the icy walls of Winter's castle under the silent gaze of the frozen suitors. The dark forest filled with whispers and wails as they darted from tree to tree, hoping not to be seen by Winter's ice gremlins. Suddenly, a gust of frigid wind swept over them, shaking icicles from the barren trees and sending a whirling fury of snowflakes into the air. With a thunderous howl, Winter appeared before them.

"Did you really think you could betray me?" he hissed, his cold blue eyes blazing as Olwen and Jardur trembled before him. "See if you can escape now!" he roared, and raising his arms, he hurled a terrible blizzard at them. Stinging winds whipped blinding snow and needle-sharp icicles

down upon them as they tried to run away. And with a final, mocking laugh, Winter disappeared into the storm.

Olwen and Jardur helped each other along, struggling against the biting winds and pelting snow. Finally, Jardur motioned for Olwen to follow behind and hold onto his cloak so that he could shield her from the worst of the blizzard's fury. The punishing winds forced Jardur to his knees again and again, but he pressed onward, reassuring Olwen every step of the way.

All at once a violent gust of wind knocked Jardur to the ground. As Olwen struggled to help him, he gestured for her to go on without him. "Never! I won't leave you!" she shouted to him over the howling winds. Then, helping him to his feet, she began to pull him along.

Just when it seemed that Olwen's strength was gone, they reached the edge of the forest and came upon a glistening lake. Exhausted, they collapsed on its shore. Moments later, Jardur let out a weary sigh, and when Olwen looked into his beautiful green eyes, she saw that the light had gone out of them.

"No!" cried Olwen, and she took him in her arms, cradling him like a child. "You cannot die, my dearest Jardur!" Then she embraced him and kissed his cheek tenderly.

In that instant, the fierce winds ceased to blow, the blizzard died away, and the sun broke through the gray clouds above. The snowdrifts around them magically disappeared, revealing a lush green countryside bursting with new leaf and colorful blossom.

Olwen marveled at the sight before her. She looked down into the lake's tranquil waters and saw her reflection, her face framed by green leaves and a cloudless blue sky. And then she gasped, for reflected beside her she saw not Jardur but the face of a handsome stranger with eyes the verdant color of spring.

"Do not be afraid, Olwen," the man said quickly. "I am still your Jardur, but your love has broken cruel Winter's spell. Spring has returned in all its glory, and at last you can see me as I truly am, young and strong."

Olwen looked lovingly into Jardur's gentle green eyes, and they held each other close as the beauty of springtime returned to all the land.

At Winter's castle, the frozen suitors sprang to life, and together they drove a defeated Winter and his ice gremlins into the far-off mountains at the edge of the world. There he was made to stay until spring's warmth softened his icy heart and he mended his selfish ways.

In time, Olwen and her siblings, Summer and Autumn, forgave their wayward brother and allowed him to return—but only for as long as a wintertime, and not a moment more.